# WAKE

By Shawn Dougherty

Illustrated by Leah Busch

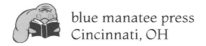 blue manatee press
Cincinnati, OH

Published by blue manatee press, Cincinnati, Ohio.
blue manatee press and associated logo
are registered trademarks of Arete Ventures, LLC.

First Edition: Fall, 2017.

Library of Congress Cataloging-In-Publication Data
*Wake* / by Shawn Dougherty; illustrated by Leah Busch—1st ed.
Summary: Awakened by his friend Owl in the quiet hours of the
night, a boy ventures out to his special place in the forest. Owl is waiting
there, along with Oak and Moon, and together they teach the boy about
the sacred power of nature to connect all things. Filled with striking
watercolor illustrations and poetic text, *Wake* is a quiet celebration of
our bond with the natural world.

ISBN-13 (hardcover): 978-1-936669-60- 8
[Juvenile Fiction- Nature & the Natural World/General. 2. Juvenile Fiction - Imagination & Play.]
Printed in the USA.

Artwork was created using pencil and watercolor.
Editorial design by Mayte Suarez.

Thank you Gary, Leah, Jesse, Ceara, and our Mother Earth, for teaching me what matters.
Thank you Kelen, Jackson, and James, for keeping me close to the earth and her creatures.
I dedicate WAKE to you and to all our children, whoever and wherever you may be.
And to KST, LKBR, BG, MD, MT, and JT, my love and gratitude
for your support, encouragement, and faith in the children of the world,
and in this story.

–SKD


Thank you, Mom, for this collaboration,
and for teaching me to cultivate my own connection to the earth
and all her living things.

–LKBR

In dream I am far away,
standing still and silent
at the edge of a mountain forest.
Moonlight has turned
the crackling snow to blue.

A distant owl call
is the only sound I hear.
Burrowing creatures dream
under the deep, deep snow.
I feel them all around me.

One small, banded feather drifts down, tickles my nose, and lands gently in the palm of my hand.

Millions of stars fill the sky.
Reaching high,
I can almost touch them.

In a flash, the northern lights swoop low,
blue, purple, a dozen shades of green.

The lights dance and swirl above my head, ruffle my hair, and send ripples of surprise all through me.

Like a river of turquoise, they carry me up in dizzy spirals.
I am light as a feather.
My heart is a pounding drum.

I hear Owl's call:
*Wake! Come meet me on our hillside.*

Tingling with excitement, I rise to join her
and open the door to the full Harvest Moon.

Moon lights my way
as I scramble up the scattered stones,

my feet flying over tiny, ancient sea creatures
who have waited here since long ago,
when this was the bottom of the sea.

Grandmother's moonflowers tickle my ankles and toes,
fragile trumpets open wide to the silver moonlight.
I breathe in their sweet, familiar scent.

I settle into my favorite place beside my fort,
my sacred space in the soft grass beneath my friend, Oak.

This is our place... Owl's, Oak's, Moon's, and *mine*.

They watch as I dig my toes into the cool, moist earth,
stirring up the musty scent of last year's leaves
and little creatures who lived here not so long ago.

I close my eyes,
breathe in...
breathe out...
and listen.

Oak whispers,

*Wake! Feel the current of the secret spring deep beneath us. The constant song of those I have sheltered, your kin, who knew me well.*

*Wake! Know every growing thing whose home we share.*
*Take comfort here, my child, my fine, true friend.*

"Come, Owl," I call.

My heart beats fast and
steady in my throat as I listen,
still and moonstruck.

Suddenly, in near silence,
Owl's wings stir the air
as she lands just above me.
I climb towards her,
and feel her wing–breath on my skin.
I hear her heartbeat...

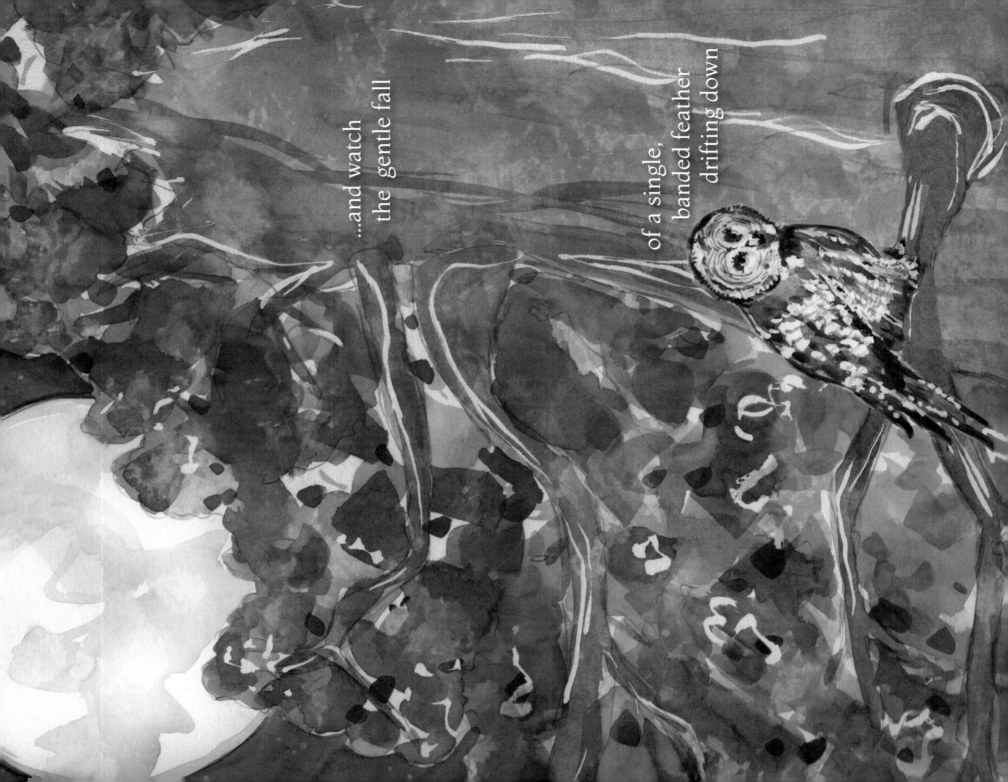

...and watch
the gentle fall

of a single,
banded feather
drifting down

into my outstretched hand.

rises... up... up...

Then, too soon,
she spreads her enormous wings,

toward the edge of the woods.

As my eyes follow her,
I see first light.

Silvery clouds in the eastern sky turn to palest yellow, then deep gold like Owl's eyes, then coral pink.

Oak's canopy glows.

Sun's light spreads
down Oak's massive trunk,
warms my moon cheeks,
and paints me golden like the sky.

Looking up into Oak's branches,
I feel part of her,
and she is part of me.

I wrap my arms around her,
hold her rough, damp bark against my cheek,
and inhale the breath of the woods.

My arms open wide to Sun,
to the day, to everything here... now and always.

I whisper to Owl,
to Oak,
to Sun
and fading Moon,

"Come! Meet me here tomorrow."

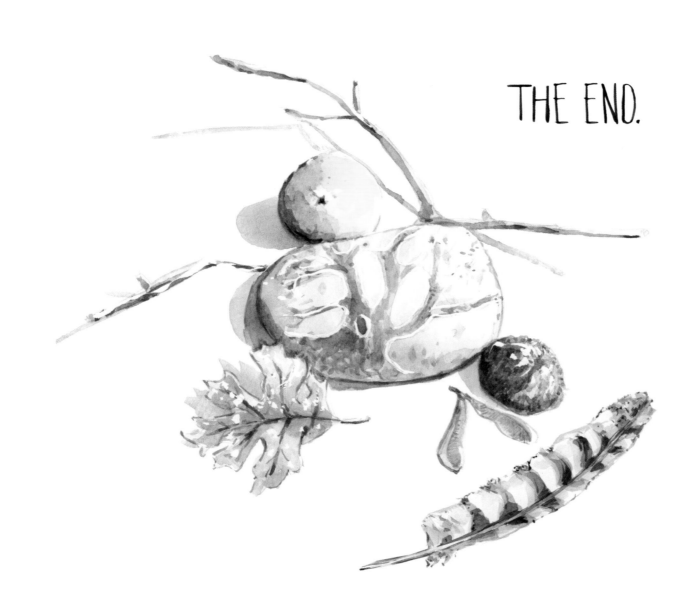

THE END.

DEAR CHILDREN,

Do you have a place outdoors where you go to daydream, listen, and think?
If so, I hope you have a sense of peace and belonging there.

Does your heart beat faster when you hear an owl call, or the sound of wind and raindrops in the trees,
or early-morning birdsong? Perhaps you've climbed, listened, and explored enough to feel the peace and connection
deep in your body, deep in your heart. Perhaps you have a special sense of living things, and know them as friends.

When I was young, I fell in love with the woods behind our house. Out there I climbed trees high enough to feel the
wind in my hair, and I surveyed my world. I set out water for the birds, then sat perfectly still so I wouldn't scare them
away. I wrote and read books aloud to myself and the trees. I wrote songs about all of it, and sang my heart out.
Things I collected there were treasures. I napped and dreamed and fell in love with the world. I could really breathe in
that place, where I knew I belonged and trusted myself the most. That feeling has never left me, and so I wrote this book
to remember these special places, and to share them with you.

DEAR GROWNUPS,

I believe in a kind of visceral intelligence, a strong sense of intuition and knowing. I have seen very young children
experience a connection with the earth and animals in that way. Guided by sensitive adults to
spend an abundance of time in nature, and to integrate their experiences, I believe all children
can come to know themselves and the earth in a deeply personal way. Care and
respect for the planet and for all living things grows from that knowing.
Parents and children grow closer, too.
May all children, of *every* age, have opportunities
to create such memories and such connections.

Do you remember?